SOMEONE WALKS BY
The Wonders of Winter Wildlife

Story and Illustration by
Polly Carlson-Voiles

Raven PRODUCTIONS, INC

ELY, MINNESOTA

Photograph on page 32 ©Jim Brandenburg

Published 2008 by Raven Productions, Inc.
P.O. Box 188, Ely, MN 55731
218-365-3375
www.ravenwords.com

Printed in Minnesota on recycled paper - 10% PCW
United States of America
10 9 8 7 6 5 4 3 2 1

Library of Congress Cataloging-in-Publication Data

Carlson-Voiles, Polly, 1943-
  Someone walks by : the wonders of winter wildlife /
by Polly Carlson-Voiles.
     p. cm.
  ISBN 978-0-9801045-5-4 (hardcover : alk. paper) —
ISBN 978-0-9801045-6-1 (softcover : alk. paper)
  1. Forest animals—Wintering—Juvenile literature.
  2. Winter—Juvenile literature. I. Title.
  QL753.C37 2008
  591.723—dc22

                                    2008036871

In memory of my mother, Alice McNear Carlson.
To Juanita and Judy.
To my best and closest: Steve, Anna and Nick.

During the night,
the deep, cold night,
the wind shakes the clouds,
loosening the snow that
feathers every stick and rock
and animal.
A thickness of white
hides the life of the forest.

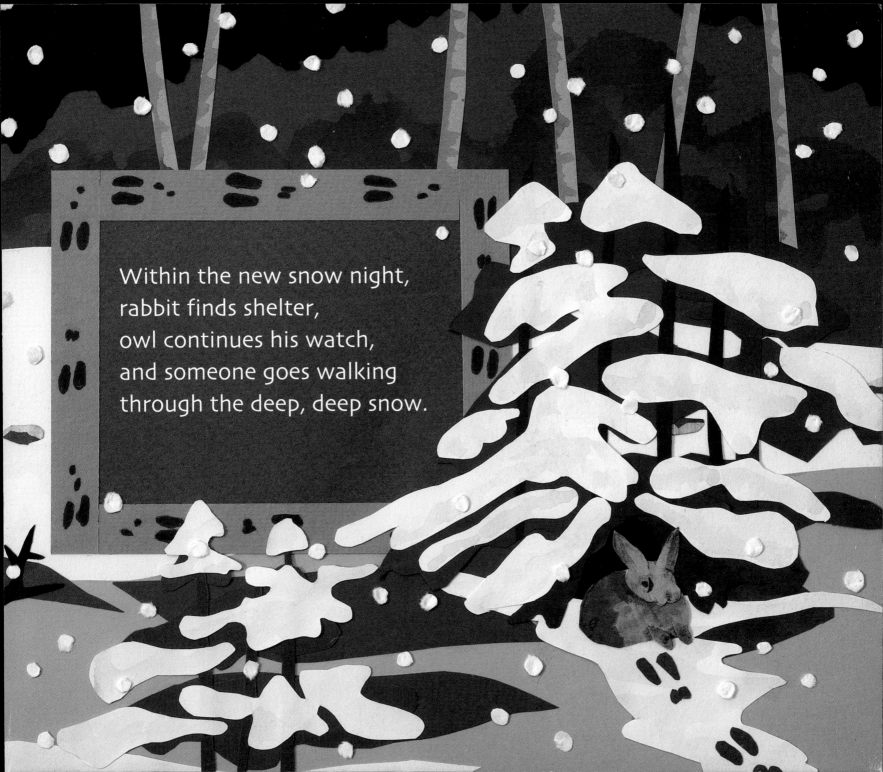

Within the new snow night,
rabbit finds shelter,
owl continues his watch,
and someone goes walking
through the deep, deep snow.

Morning dawns.
In the thin blue light of midwinter, under the gaze of jays,
almost everything is tucked into coats of white.
Otter waits while her mate swims after a sleepy fish.
Someone walks across the river ice that makes a firm lid
over the water running beneath.

At the edge of the river, wood frog is frozen, a solid miracle, waiting like the river ice to move again in spring.
Snapping turtle snoozes deep in mud, his heart a slow and lazy drum.

Who goes walking by?
Red squirrel is watchful
as she sits beside a stump
and busily eats
from her cache of seeds.

The crust of hardened snow roofs a secret world. Crystal tunnels are laced through with light from the sun. These are the pathways and pantries of busy mouse, shrew, and vole. Sharp hooves break through the crust, poking holes, bringing air and danger into this tunneled world. Hoping for dinner, a swiftly moving ermine peers down a hoof-made air shaft.

Porcupine nibbles buds,
twigs, and the inner bark
of pine. Nearby, chickadee
seeks seeds and puffs against
the cold. Someone walks across
a wind-fallen tree. Footsteps
softened by snow do not disturb
bear in her deep, deep sleep,
snuggled with her cubs,
each small enough to curl in the
palms of two human hands.

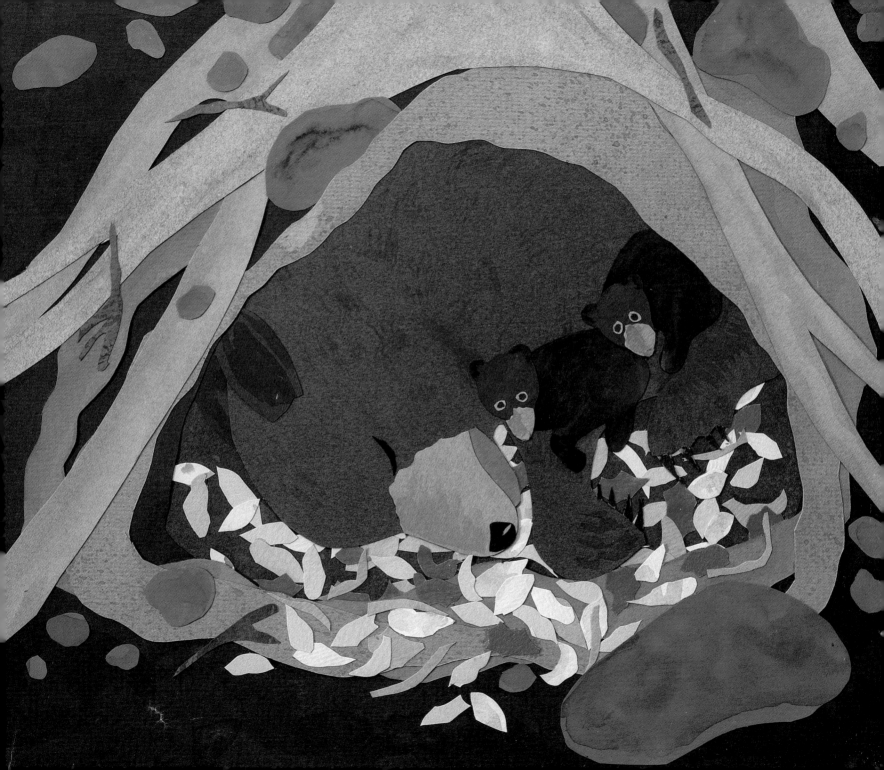

Someone walks across a ledge of granite. Lynx crouches on his hunting bed, a shelf of sun-warmed rock, waiting for his favorite prey. Snowshoe hare makes herself a shadow beneath a whitened bush, brave in her winter dress, holding jittery quickness still, stone still.

Secure deep within the rock,
in a thin and perfect cave,
little brown bat and friends
snuggle and shiver together
in their winter sleep.

Past a thatched lodge of mud and sticks,
someone walks down the river. Mink
looks for open water, a crayfish in mind.
Pileated woodpecker drills for insects
sleeping in the trees.

Inside their living room, the beaver and their kits huddle together. The kits lunch on tasty bark peeled from branches piled and jammed into a cache in fall, stored for the ice time. Adults live mostly on fat stored in their rounded bodies and tails.

Someone walks into the woods along a marshy shore, over logs and into taller trees. She sniffs at tracks well known to her, two-toed tracks larger than her own. Later, moose returns, eager to browse on the young twigs of mountain maple and willow.

In his leaf-lined
underground rooms,
chipmunk twirls in dreams,
awakening only to eat,
sleeping on a dinner pile
of nuts and seeds.

Night has come again and someone continues on her way. She stops, dips her nose, smells smaller two-toes. But she has something else to do, something pulling her. Alert, deer listen in their winter yards, trim cedar trees, nip the tender pine seedlings, eat the newest growth of dogwood.

Flying squirrel sails,
lands on snow and slides,
hurrying to his home
with friends in an
abandoned woodpecker
hole. Skunk takes
week-long naps,
wakens to stroll and eat,
then naps again.

Someone crosses the edge of a clearing.
Close to his den, fox hunts,
diving headfirst into snow.
Nearby, a paper wasps' nest hangs
like an ornament, empty of life.

Beneath the snow, garter snakes curl
in deep cracks in the earth. In the fall
they slithered for miles to clump
together below the frost line.
Queen hornet lies here, too,
heavy with the responsibility
of creating her kind anew in spring.

The deepest cold explodes a tree. Someone walking here goes quietly with a watchful eye. The smell is here, the noisy ones to run from. Birds decorate the trees and snow with flashes of rose, yellow, and blue. Woodpecker's hammering rings from tree to tree.

The two-footed ones and their four-footed friend
are warming by the fire. Smoke rises from their den.
Nose testing the air, someone slips quietly by.

Light thins.
Raven shouts his
hoarse announcement
from the
tallest
tree.

"Kruk, Tok!
Someone's
coming!
Take care!
Look!
Someone's
coming!!"

Grouse plunges headlong into a bank of snow and squirms her way down inside. Here the warmth of her body will ice the snow into a cozy igloo, protecting her from the dangerous ones.

Someone senses the time is now.
She stops to howl across the lake.
Light shreds into pinks and blues
and greens, slowly soaked up by
the darker blue of coming night.
Her hollow tone colors the air,
starts low, slides up like a saxophone,
then dips to wait like a question.
The "I am here!" song of winter.

Across the lake,
a thinner distant howl replies,
clear as a clarinet,
stronger than wind.
Its melody climbs again and again.
"I am here, too!" his answer sings.
Darkness sinks down
to hug the earth again.

Someone runs
to meet her mate.
Stars appear.
The buttery moon
gets tangled in the trees. Ice cracks and booms with cold.

Two wolves run and dance on moonlit paws,
racing with shoulders pressed together.
Flowing in the touch and smell of each other,
free in what they've always known.

A few of the amazing facts about animals in winter

Snow helps and hinders animals. Soft snow allows the ruffed grouse to burrow. Snow that melts from ground warmth is called pukak and allows mice to tunnel. Deep-crusted snow, called upsik, can trap the legs of deer, but supports the weight of smaller animals. Snow insulates, providing a blanket that traps warmth. Heavy snow on trees, called qali, limits access to food by covering seeds and cones. Chickadees hang upside down to get seeds from cones covered by qali. Otters can breathe in an air space between ice and water. They have two entrances to their riverbank dens, one underwater and one above the ground. Fish supercool, moving very little when they are in near-freezing water, for movement can cause ice crystals to form inside their cells. Wood frogs freeze into frogsicles by moving sugars from their livers to form a protective solution that prevents cells from rupturing. These sugars return to the frogs' livers when they thaw in spring. Mice find food and warmth in tunnels under the snow. Shrews and voles tunnel under the ground and come up for food. Deer and moose shed antlers in winter. Mice and other rodents chew up antlers for calcium, sometimes devouring them completely. Bear cubs are born during hibernation. Their mother can make a furry tent for them by sleeping on her elbows. A bear's temperature does not drop like some hibernating animals. During hibernation, adult bears eat nothing and recycle all their waste products. Lynx live almost entirely on a diet of snowshoe hares. Some bats migrate, but little brown bats hibernate in caves or wells. Adult beavers live on fat stored in their tails and body. The branches stowed underwater in mud are primarily for their yearlings to eat. Both moose and wolves have antifreeze-like fat in hoofs and paws. Chipmunks lower their body temperature and sleep the winter away. Since they can't put on enough fat, they sleep on piles of seeds and nuts they've stored, and occasionally awaken to eat. Deer gather, providing safety in numbers. They pack down trails in the snow where there is plenty of the brush they prefer for browse. Their thin legs sink into the deep snow if they move out of these yards. During the coldest times, skunks, squirrels, and porcupines take long winter naps, sometimes having slumber parties to share warmth. Other times they are active and hunt for food. Foxes pair up in late fall and dig a den. Some reptiles, amphibians, and insects dig down beneath the frost level in the ground where they become dormant. Many insect species have a queen who is the only one of her group to survive winter. She lays eggs in spring. Turtles sleep down in the mud. Some snakes travel as far as 11 miles to heap up with other snakes in an underground hibernaculum, a well or deep crack in the ground. Severe cold can explode trees, sounding like gunshots, if the trees freeze all the way through. Ravens are the newscasters of the woods. They are scavengers, cleaning up scraps left by predators. Wolves lose very little heat through their fur, even in the coldest cold, as long as they curl up and cover their faces with their fluffed tails. Their challenge in the winter is to find enough food. It can be difficult to chase and catch prey in deep snow. If separated, wolves will travel far to join their packs again.

You can learn more and find other resources at www.ravenwords.com under Lesson Plans.

wolf track image by Jim Brandenburg